Isabelle Wilson...

CONTENTS

The Human ZOO

Virginia Ironside

Illustrations by
Caroline Holden

WALKER BOOKS
LONDON

For
Zoocheck
Dorking
Surrey RH5 6HA

First published 1991 by
Walker Books Ltd, 87 Vauxhall Walk
London SE11 5HJ

Text © 1991 Virginia Ironside
Illustrations © 1991 Caroline Holden

Printed and bound in Great Britain by
Richard Clay Ltd, Bungay, Suffolk

British Library Cataloguing in Publication Data
Ironside, Virginia
The human zoo.
I. Title   II. Holden, Caroline
823'.914 [F]
ISBN 0-7445-2068-1

school. They were waiting for some wounded animal to pass by so they could swoop on it and eat it. I thought they were waiting for me and I ran all the way home."

"Swoop, swoop!" yelled Darren, flapping his arms over his plate and picking up a bit of meat with his teeth. "I'm a vulture!"

"They were nice in *The Jungle Book*," said Mum, making conversation and trying not to look at Darren.

"And in *Dumbo*," said Tricia. "They helped Dumbo fly, remember? They sang that song."

"Those were crows," said Paul, scornfully. "And anyway, they won't be singing in the zoo. And they won't be wearing clothes either. When I grow up I want to be a zoo-keeper and look after the animals."

"Bit of a smelly job," said Tricia, helping herself to the last of the sprouts.

"Hold on," said Mum. "Maybe Darren would like some more. Ask him first."

"Vultures don't like sprouts," said Darren flapping his arms again.

"You'd have to clean out the animals' cages, Paul," said his dad. "And feed them live mice and things like that."

"And it's not a very well-paid job," said his mum, as she began to clear away the plates. "And it's dangerous."

"But all the animals would like me," said Paul. "I'd be their best zoo-keeper. I'd be their friend."

"They'd probably bite off your arm the minute you offered them something to eat," said Tricia. "And think of wading through elephants' poo every day."

"Elephants' poo!" said Darren, horrified. "Think how big it would be! And their wee! They probably wee gallons and gallons every day!"

"Darren!" said Mum, making a face.

"Darren's the guest," said Tricia. "He can say what he likes."

Paul felt terribly excited as they got near the zoo. The distant sound of the trumpeting of an elephant sent shivers down his spine – and he could hear the parrots cawing and a strange "whrrmphing" sound of an animal he couldn't identify. When they got in, the first thing Paul noticed was how big the zoo was – and the second thing he noticed was the smell.

"Definitely elephants' poo," said Darren, knowledgeably.

It was very hot and, being a Sunday afternoon, crammed with families all wandering around eating ice-creams and staring into glass windows and cages. Dad had bought a plan and he sat on a concrete flower pot as he pored over it.

"What first?" he said.

"The monkeys!" said Paul. Ever since he'd seen Cheetah, the monkey in the old black and white Tarzan films on telly, he'd always longed for a monkey of his own.

And after they'd walked for ages through concrete underpasses, past cages of strange birds and animals and past cafés full of screaming kids, they finally got to the monkey cages.

"Look at them!" said Tricia. "Oh, there's a baby one! Aren't they sweet!"

A whole family of monkeys seemed to be living in the one cage. Some were sitting on bare branches, one was picking fleas out of another's coat and a big old one came up and stared at them all through the bars, making chattering noises.

"He's talking to us!" said Paul. "Listen!"

"Of course he's not talking to us," said Darren. "He's just gibbering. Gibber, gibber."

"We don't know how they communicate," said Dad. "But he seems to be saying something, doesn't he? No doubt when you're a zoo-keeper, Paul, you'll be able to understand what they mean!"

"He already acts like a monkey," said Tricia scornfully. Paul was just about to stick out his tongue at her when he noticed the big old monkey was watching them intently. It seemed to be listening to them. But then – it couldn't be, surely?

They stayed for a while watching the monkeys springing through the branches and shaking their fists and chasing each other; then Mum said she wanted to have a proper look at the giraffes.

"I'll catch you up," said Paul. He wanted to stay and watch the monkeys for a bit longer. They had such lovely long brown fingers and their little ears were so neat, tucked tidily into the sides of their head. He loved their big brown eyes and their funny curved mouths. This trip to the zoo, he decided, was the best birthday present he'd had. He *certainly* would become a zoo-keeper when he grew up, whatever anyone said.

He was just about to turn away to catch up with the rest of his family when the big monkey started chattering to him again through the bars. Paul stared back for a minute.

And then something most peculiar happened. The monkey put one of its long brown hands into its fur and pulled it out again, its fist closed. Then it reached out its long arm to Paul through the bars, as if offering him something.

As there was a big notice saying "Don't touch the monkeys!" Paul kept his hands to his sides. But the monkey persisted. It kept chattering and chattering and stretching its long brown arm further and further towards Paul as if pleading with him to take something. Paul looked round. There was no one about. No one would see. Nervously, he stretched out his hand. The monkey grabbed it, turned it over – and into it placed three peanuts.

"Come off it!" said Paul, as he took them. "We're meant to be feeding *you*, not the other way round!" He was about to put the peanuts into his pocket when the monkey started chattering even more noisily than before. And now, with a long brown finger, it mimed putting peanuts into its mouth.

"You want *me* to eat them?" said Paul.

The monkey nodded, but held up one finger.

"Just one?"

The monkey nodded again.

"OK," said Paul. There could be no harm in it. He took a peanut from his palm, ate it, and put the other two into his pocket.

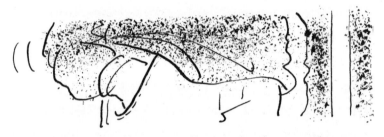

"Happy now?" he said to the monkey.

And, to his utter astonishment, the monkey replied "Yes".

Paul was struck dumb. He just couldn't believe his ears. He looked around to see if anyone else had joined him, but he was still completely alone. He turned back to the cage, goggling at the monkey who'd just spoken to him.

"*What* did you say?" said Paul.

"I said 'Yes'," replied the monkey. "Those are magic peanuts. Whenever you eat one you can understand what animals are saying and they can understand you, too. They only last a day, so use them sparingly."

"But why me?" said Paul, stunned. "Why give them to me?"

"Because you said you wanted to be a zoo-keeper when you grow up. And I want to tell you that's not a nice job to have because lots of animals in zoos are very unhappy. You ask the other animals. Then you'll change your mind. In the mean time I'm stuck here like a prisoner with the others."

"A prisoner? Don't you like it here?" said Paul. "You get all your meals, you're well looked after."

The monkey shook its head. "Honestly, are you a complete wally?" it asked.

Paul felt a bit cross. He'd never been called a wally by a monkey before. Of course he'd never been called *anything* by a monkey before.

"All we want to do," said the monkey, wistfully, "is to be back in the wild, looking for fruit in the tops of trees. We want to see the clouds in the sky and feel the rain on our fur. We want to see the seasons changing, we want to build our own fresh nests out of leaves and twigs each night. And instead we're trapped for the whole of our lives in this steel prison." And with that the monkey turned sadly on its heel, walked back over the concrete floor and climbed on to a bare branch where it sat gloomily examining its fur.

Paul couldn't believe his ears. He ran back to his family who were looking at the giraffes.

"Mum! Dad! I can understand what the animals are saying!" he said. "They hate it! It's cruel!"

But at that moment a giraffe came ambling up to him. "They'll never believe you," it said. "Don't try to explain."

Paul stared up at it. "So don't *you* like it here either?"

The giraffe opened its mouth and said, tetchily, "Like it? Like it? How would *you* like it? In the wild we'd go for great races in the sunshine with thirty or forty of our friends, stretching up to nibble the tender young tops of trees. Here we can only go a few measly paces on the concrete, and day after day all we see is that cafeteria over there and a small patch of sky."

Tricia turned to Paul. "Did you speak to that giraffe?" she said. "You ought to be locked up in a loony bin. I knew you were bats."

"Bats, bats," said Darren, flapping his arms again.

Paul was glad when his dad suggested seeing the polar bear – and then he had second thoughts. He couldn't face any more complaints.

"We'll get some ice-lollies," said his mum.

As they made their way to the polar bear enclosure, licking their ice-lollies, Paul wished he'd never eaten the magic peanut. After all,

this whole trip was meant to be a treat – he'd
come here to enjoy himself, not to be made to
feel frightful by every animal he met.

The bear was sitting on top of a rock,
swaying its head backwards and forwards.
When it saw Paul's ice-lolly it sauntered up.
"Ah, ice," it said, enviously. "You're so lucky
to have some ice."

"Don't go on," muttered Paul under his breath so his family wouldn't hear. "I don't want to know. It's my birthday. I'm here to have some fun."

But the polar bear wouldn't shut up. "Fun! Fun!" it wailed. "The last time I had fun was when I used to swim for miles and miles among the ice-floes of the Arctic." Paul could see that the only water the bear had was a soupy pool with a few sweet-papers floating in it. "And when I was a cub we used to roll down the snow-slopes with our mum watching, and here I am all on my own for ever and ever." A tear rolled out of its eye.

"Look, he's crying," said Tricia excitedly.

"No he's not," said Paul's dad. "Bears don't cry, they don't feel things like us." Paul was about to interrupt when Darren said, "Can we go to the dolphinarium? The dolphins do great tricks! It said the show was at four!"

Paul felt his heart sinking into his boots. He looked at his watch. Ten to four. Surely they could go home soon? He didn't want to stay here a minute longer. He was about to say he had a tummy ache when Tricia squealed, "Oh please, please!" so there was no getting out of it. All he could hope, as he followed his family morosely to the dolphinarium, was that it would be too late to get tickets.

To get to the dolphinarium, you had to walk through the aquarium, a dark, steamy, murky place, the silence broken only by the sound of the humming of aquarium bubblers. Thank goodness, thought Paul – at least if the fish did speak he wouldn't be able to hear what they had to say through the water.

For a moment Paul thought he'd be spared the show because the man at the ticket booth shouted, "Sold out! Next show at five!" but his relief was short-lived. Just beyond the booth, his father was triumphantly waving the last five tickets. There was no getting out of it now. He just couldn't upset his dad when he'd gone to all this trouble – so Paul sat down reluctantly in the back row of the seats, hoping the dolphins couldn't see him in the dark.

The dolphinarium was just a big swimming pool with five dolphins splashing about in it. When the trainer came on and threw some fish into the water, they started jumping through hoops, catching balls and leaping out of the water. Now *they* looked happy enough, thought Paul. After all, if they weren't happy they wouldn't do tricks.

At the end of the show, the trainer suddenly spoke through a microphone. "Now, girls and boys, is there anyone here with a birthday?" he asked. Several children were shoved forward by their parents. "Go on," said Mum. "It's your birthday. Go on up."

Now if there was one thing Paul *didn't* want to do it was go anywhere near those dolphins, but Mum pushed him affectionately to the side of the pool.

"Hello, boys and girls," said the trainer. He was a rather greasy man in a dirty tracksuit. "First of all, the dolphins would like to make your acquaintance!" Gingerly, Paul stared over the side; a dolphin came up to him.

"Don't speak to me," whispered Paul. "I don't want to hear anything more." But the dolphin looked at him so pleadingly that he relented. "Oh, OK. But *surely* you're happy? You're doing great tricks!"

"Tricks, tricks! We *hate* doing tricks day after day!" said the dolphin.

"But you're smiling," said Paul, looking closely at its mouth which was curved into a happy grin.

"That's the way our mouths are shaped," sighed the dolphin. "Inside we're not a bit happy. The chlorine hurts our eyes and it's all too noisy for our sensitive ears. We just want to get back to the big, blue ocean. Is there anything you can do for us? Please?"

But before Paul could reply, the trainer interrupted. "And now, the dolphins will sing 'Happy Birthday' for you!" he said. A crackly old tape-recorder started up the first strains of "Happy Birthday to You" – the trainer clapped his hands as a signal for the dolphins to come into the centre of the pool. Paul's dolphin went off slowly, muttering, "Back to work!" Then the dolphins started singing.

To the audience it really did sound as if they were singing "Happy Birthday". But Paul heard a different song.

"We want to be free,
We want to be free,
We long for the ocean,
We want to be free!"

Paul was so upset he just dashed away, out of the dophinarium. He couldn't stand being in that place one minute longer.

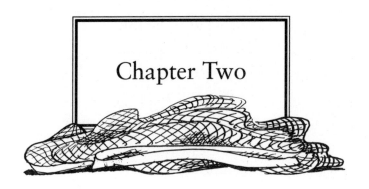

Chapter Two

Gasping in the humid darkness, Paul looked
frantically for the EXIT sign. He just had to
get out of the zoo as quickly as possible. If
he'd known what it was going to be like he'd
never have asked to come. Finally spotting
the way out, he rushed from the aquarium
and into the open air, panting in the sunshine.
Desperately he searched for more signs. He'd
just run and run until he got to the exit and
then he'd wait till his family found him and
he'd pretend he'd got lost. And then he'd go
home and try to forget about all the horrible
things he'd heard.

When he spotted a notice saying EXIT, he

saw it had two other words written on it –
EAGLES and LIONS. Paul looked round for
a different way out, but that was the only
path. And as he tried to sprint past the eagles'
cage, one sharp-eyed eagle spotted him.

"Paul, Paul," it squawked, waving its huge
wings. "Why are you rushing? Don't you
want to hear how *I* feel?"

"No," said Paul, feeling awful as he said it. "I've heard quite enough already thank you. I've got to go."

"That's a pity," said the eagle. It was sitting gloomily on a long metal pole. "You listen to everyone else, but you don't want to listen to me. Thanks a bunch."

Paul hesitated. "It's not that I don't want … well, quite honestly, I don't think I can *bear* to hear any more," he said, apologetically.

"That's a stupid thing to say," said the eagle. "If everyone thought like you, then how would any good come out of the world? You can't just block your ears to it. You've got to listen, even if you don't do anything about it."

"OK," sighed Paul, stopping at the cage and staring up at the glorious bird. "I'm listening."

"If I could only describe to you," said the eagle, "the feeling of soaring high in the sky, with the wind whistling through my flight feathers as I used to fly over plains and hills

and valleys and cliffs looking for prey, you'd know how I feel now. Here, I can see the sky through my cage bars, but I can't get up there. I can't even flap my wings more than a few times. I would give anything, anything, to get out of here."

"I'm very sorry," mumbled Paul. "I wish I could do something."

"So do I," said the eagle.

"Could I open your cage maybe so you could fly away?" said Paul.

"What good would it do me?" said the eagle crossly. "I couldn't fly back to the wild. It's too far away and anyway, I'm too old."

Giving him a sad and sympathetic smile, Paul shuffled off feeling wretched.

Only the lions to go, now. Maybe he could crawl past their cage on his hands and knees so they wouldn't see him. Then they wouldn't be able to speak to him.

But he'd just dropped to his knees when one of the lions shouted, "Stop! I can smell you! Get up!"

Sheepishly, Paul got to his feet and brushed himself down. "Well, you're OK, aren't you?" he said, looking at the bit of grass the lion was sitting on – and seeing the hunk of fresh meat nearby.

"OK? OK?" snapped the lion. "If you knew what it was like to lie on a rock on the plain just watching the herds of antelope go by, if you knew what it was like sitting in the sun or lying in the shade of an acacia tree in the middle of the day, then using my camouflage to stalk my prey, using my strength and speed to catch my supper and bring it back to my family, if you knew what it was like to be lord of all I surveyed … then you'd never say this was 'OK' as you call it. I

can't run anywhere. I'm trapped. I hope," he said to Paul, "that *you* never have the experience of being trapped in a zoo."

"Well," said Paul, "I suppose I might go to prison one day…" He didn't think he would but you never knew.

"Prison! Prison! Prison's a punishment for doing wrong!" roared the lion. "I've done no one any harm in my life! And anyway, hardly anyone stays in prison for ever. They always come out one day. I'm here for the rest of my life and I'll never see my home again." And with this, the great beast put his great big yellow head between his great big paws and heaved a great big sigh like a sob.

"I – I'm awfully sorry," said Paul, seeing the exit out of the corner of his eye. "But I've got to go. My family will be worried."

As the lion didn't look up, he tiptoed past to the exit. Going to the zoo had been the most horrible experience in his whole life. And what on earth would he say to his mum and dad who'd organized all this for him specially? He looked at his watch. He hoped they'd be out soon. He couldn't bear to wait here for long because all he could hear in the air was the sounds of animals crying and wailing for help and begging to be released.

"Where have you been?" said everyone when they found him. "We've been worried sick about you!"

"I was just looking around on my own," said Paul. "I'm sorry. I lost you in the dolphinarium."

His mother was about to launch into a big ticking off but Paul's dad stopped her. "Come on, it's his birthday," he said. "This was his treat and as long as he's seen the zoo and enjoyed it, that's fine. We all had a good time, didn't we?"

"Brill!" said Darren. "I loved the dolphins doing their tricks."

"And the lions were great!" said Tricia.

"And the kangaroos were sweet!" said Mum.

"And the vultures were marvellous," said

his dad. "And I certainly prefer seeing them behind bars to seeing them in the wild."

As they walked to the car Paul didn't know what to say. He couldn't say he'd enjoyed it because he hadn't, so he just mumbled, "Well, thank you very much for taking me. It was very interesting." Which was true because it had been – but it had been interesting in all the wrong ways.

As they drove further away from the zoo, Paul started to feel a bit better. From the back seat he leant over his dad's shoulder.

"Don't you think it's rather cruel, keeping them cooped up like that?"

His mother laughed. "Cruel? They live a life of luxury! They're well looked after. They've got no meals to cook. No washing-up to do. No shopping. All their needs catered for – I wouldn't mind living in a zoo, I can tell you!"

"Nor me!" said his father. "No work to go to. No bills to pay. A perpetual holiday. A life of Riley."

"I wish I lived in a zoo," said Darren bouncing up and down beside him. "No school. I'd make faces at people all day long."

"Don't be so stupid," said Paul, crossly.

"I'm not stupid," said Darren.

"Oh, shut up," snapped Paul.

"Now Paul, don't tell people to shut up, it's rude," said his mum.

"Sorry," said Paul in a bad-tempered way.

Tricia was still wondering about living in a zoo. "Well, as long as it was a *nice* zoo I wouldn't mind. But I wouldn't like people staring at me all the time."

"Well I wish you *could* all live in a zoo," said Paul, angrily. "Then you'd see what it was *really* like!"

"Fat chance of that, I'm afraid," said Mum as they got home and she got out of the car. "OK, who's for some tea? I'm starving!"

"Me too," said Darren. "Come on Paul. Cheer up. We can watch telly and then we can play with those cars of yours and then..."

But Paul didn't feel like eating tea. He didn't feel like watching telly. He didn't feel like doing anything. He just couldn't get what he'd heard at the zoo out of his head.

Later, when he undressed, he remembered the two remaining magic peanuts and was tempted to throw them away. He never wanted to be able to understand animals' conversations again. But as he was looking at the nuts, wondering what to do with them, Mum popped into his bedroom to say goodnight – so he quickly slipped them into his pyjama pocket in case she saw them. He

said goodnight to Darren, who had bedded
down on the floor beside him in a sleeping
bag, and tried to sleep.

Perhaps in the morning he'd have forgotten
all about it. He tossed and turned for what
seemed like hours, his mind whirring with all
the events of the day, until he finally fell into
a fitful doze. He dreamed of elephants in
ballet dresses, of clowns dressed up as
pantomime horses, of rabbits eating breakfast

with knives and forks, of carnival people dressed as strange birds … until he was woken by a strange rustling and bumping sound outside his window. He rubbed his eyes, sat up and looked out.

Through the darkness he could just make out what seemed to be a net hanging outside the window pane. He stared closer. The net was moving slightly – and it looked as if it was made out of grass. Impossible, thought Paul. And why would anyone put it there? What on *earth* could it be?

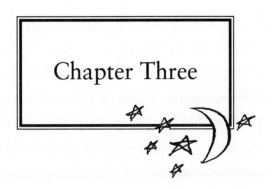

Chapter Three

Leaning down from his bed, Paul shook
Darren awake with a trembling hand. His
heart was thumping and as Darren woke up
with a grunt, he whispered, "Sssh!"

"What's the matter?" said Darren rather
crossly. He checked his watch. "Paul, it's four
in the morning!"

"There's something funny going on,"
whispered Paul. "Can't you hear the noise?
And look at that – what is it?" He pointed to
the window. "I think it's burglars!"

"I can't see properly, it's not light enough
yet," said Darren, rubbing his eyes. But he
climbed out of his sleeping bag and got up on

to Paul's bed to examine the window. "Oh – I see," he added as he noticed the net. "Are you sure it isn't there normally? Mightn't it be something your dad put up to get ivy or roses or something to grow over? My dad's got kind of netting up the side of the house to train some plants."

Paul frowned. He didn't remember his dad putting up anything like that. Or maybe it had always been there above his window and had slipped down in the night. He peered out of the window again. Then, through the net he made out some funny shapes at the end of the path, and a big horse-drawn wagon parked in the road.

"Who are they?" he said, staring. "Do you think they're gypsies?"

Darren screwed up his eyes. "They don't look like people," he said, nervously. "They're too big."

There was a long frightened silence as the two boys peered out. Then Darren said, all in a rush but not wanting to sound too scared,

"Let's go and wake your mum and dad. I don't like the look of them." Then he added, rather accusingly, "This never happens at *our* house."

Though Paul knew Mum and Dad would hate being woken, if it was Darren who was waking them, they couldn't mind too much. After all, he was a guest and Paul remembered another friend had once got frightened in the night and Mum hadn't minded at all when he wanted to be taken home even though it was three in the morning. Or rather she'd grumbled a lot when she got home but she hadn't said anything at the time.

Mum and Dad were both fast asleep but Paul shook Mum awake. "What's the matter?" she said sleepily.

"What time is it?" said Paul's dad crossly, waking up and looking at his watch. "It's the middle of the night! Go back to sleep!"

But Darren was too frightened to budge. He stood in the darkness shivering in his pyjamas. "We're sorry to wake you," he said nervously, "but there are some horrible people – well, kind of things – outside, and there's a net over our window."

Paul glanced at Mum and Dad's window. "Look!" he said, pointing. "There's the same thing here. It's like a trap!"

"Trap!" said Paul's dad crossly, reaching for his glasses and stumbling out of bed. "You're having nightmares." He shuffled angrily over to the window – and Paul heard his sharp intake of breath.

"You're right!" he said, peering out. "There *is* a weird net over the window! And it looks as if it's over the whole house, too, so we can't get out! And look – what are those creatures down at the end of the path? They're coming towards us! Get up, love! Wake Tricia! I'll call the police! Now, everyone, keep quiet and don't panic!"

Without putting on his dressing gown he hurried out of the door and ran down the stairs to the phone. But before he reached it, there was a crashing at the door and the sound of splintering wood.

"They're breaking the door down!" cried Mum, turning on the light. "Quick, kids, hide!"

Paul's heart was beating so hard he could hardly hear himself think. The noise downstairs was getting louder and louder and was accompanied by the most awful grunts and roars.

Pulling Darren after him he rushed back to his bedroom, pushed Darren into his old toy cupboard and dived under his bed. From downstairs came the most frightful yelling – followed by his father shouting, "Help me! Help me! Police!"

After that it was chaos. It all happened so quickly. Mum started screaming at the top of her voice, and then Tricia rushed to her door and yelled as well. Seconds afterwards, his mum screamed some more and there was the

sound of heavy footsteps. Then Mum's voice became muffled and Paul could hear an awful bumping on the stairs, as if she were being pulled down step by step. Then there was a final shriek, "Tricia, ring the police!"

followed by silence as the door banged shut. Paul heard Tricia's door creak open as she tiptoed along the hall into his room. "Paul?" she whispered. "Darren? What's happening?"

"Hide!" whispered Paul. But at that moment the front door opened again and there were more footsteps – footsteps, this time, which were coming up the stairs. Or rather, they weren't like ordinary footsteps because there was a scratching sound at each step as if the creatures had claws. Or talons. Then Paul's own door burst open

–48–

and, to his horror, from under the bed he saw
six legs coming into the room. Four were
covered with matted fur and ended with
paws; two were grey and thin and covered
with scales. At the bottom were two huge
webbed feet.

Loud grunts and roars followed and then a
cry from Tricia. "Help me!" she cried – and
Paul saw her legs disappear as one of the
creatures lifted her up. "The animals are
taking me away!"

The four furry legs padded from the room, leaving only the two scaly legs behind. Paul and Darren remained quiet as mice. Sweat popped out over Paul's forehead and he felt sick. Then "Cawcaw – squaaawk!" said scaly-legs.

Paul saw it moving over to the cupboard and opening it. It must have covered Darren's mouth, because all Paul could see or hear were his friend's feet drumming on the floor. Paul could hardly breathe. The other creature came back without Tricia and spent a while in the bedroom, grunting and growling. Finally both animals seemed satisfied they'd

got everyone because they dragged Darren
out of the room and bumped him, too, down
the stairs – and when the door shut there was
a finality about it which made Paul feel a
little bit safer.

But even so it was a good few minutes
before he dared wriggle from under the bed.
He tiptoed to the landing, crept softly
downstairs and peeped through the letter-box.

In the early light he could make out a huge
barred wagon, and on to the front were
climbing the two creatures – one a gigantic
pelican and the other an enormous tiger. But
when the tiger took up the reins of the horses

and gave it a friendly twitch, nothing happened. One of the horses seemed to have got a hoof stuck in a bit of broken paving. This gave Paul a chance to risk opening the door a crack and slipping down the garden path. While the two animals were helping to free the horse, Paul crept stealthily round to the back of the wagon. The two heavy doors were bolted and there was no sign of Darren or his family – except for a piece of his mum's nightdress that had been caught and stuck out rather pathetically. But before he could knock on the doors or speak, the animals grunted and climbed back on to their seats. The wagon wheels started to turn very slowly, crunching on the gravel of the drive. Without a second thought, Paul leapt up and clung for dear life to the two handles on the back doors. And as the wagon started down the road, he gradually winched himself up on to the roof and slid along carefully till he was hanging directly over the two animals in front.

"Urrgh," said the tiger to the pelican. "Grr-ow!"

"Kwaaah!" replied the pelican. They seemed to be having an animal conversation.

If only he could understand what they were saying! But then Paul remembered. His magic peanuts! He'd eaten one – but he still had two left.

Slipping his hand into his pocket, he took the second peanut out and popped it into his mouth. And the moment he swallowed it he could understand every word the animals were saying.

"Good haul," said the tiger. "A whole family, too."

"Yup," said the pelican. "We'll advertise them tomorrow, get a whole lot of visitors and make a fortune. You know, this whole thing is a great idea of yours, pelican. And that girl's a good catch, isn't she? That blonde hair's quite something."

"Now, now," said one of the horses in front, turning its head back slightly. "You know there's a law against cutting blonde hair. It's getting too scarce."

"No one would know. We could kill her and say it was old hair got before the law was passed," said the pelican petulantly.

"Come on, there'd be no point in that," said the tiger. "She's young. We can use her to breed and make much more out of her."

"The mother would do for breeding, wouldn't she?"

"No, she's far too old. We can get the girl breeding with the young lad and then we'll be away."

On and on they drove, far out into the country. They rode on over plains and deserts, across vast wastes of ice and snow and empty wilderness and through rocky mountain passes. They skimmed over ranges of hills, beside great lakes and rivers, across verdant prairies and empty wastelands. Finally, they reached an extraordinary country. But it was a country that Paul had never been taught about in geography lessons.

Here there were palm trees, and great blue pools and vast plains with herds of antelope ambling through the grass. Landscapes of desert seemed to exist alongside lush meadows and jungle. Parrots and big rare butterflies flew around in the air and, in the distance, rhinos and elephants grazed. And yet there were rivers full of freezing ice-floes, with seals and polar bears playing on the banks, while tigers and kangaroos rested together near by in the baking sun.

Paul could hardly take all this in – particularly as he had to concentrate hard just to hang on to the roof of the wagon. The ride was so bumpy, he kept worrying he'd fall off. They were now entering a jungle and the

wagon plunged into the undergrowth. On the roof, Paul was at risk of being brushed off by the hanging branches of trees and palms, but he managed to hold on until, after a few miles, the wagon slowed down and came to a halt in a clearing.

"I could do with a drink," said the tiger, climbing out of the driving seat and padding down to a cool blue pool in a glade.

"So could I," said one of the horses, slipping itself from the reins and trotting down to the water.

"I'll just stretch my wings if you don't mind," said the pelican. And it was then that Paul got frightened – because he knew that the minute the pelican flew into the air, it would spot him on the top of the wagon. Wriggling as quickly as he could, he managed to slither down the side of the wagon without either animal seeing him. Then, just before the animals could catch sight of him, Paul scampered deep into the jungle, through the branches, jumping over streams, squelching through swamps, tripping over logs – running as fast as his legs would carry him.

Chapter Four

Night was falling when Paul stopped running and found a clearing of moss and sticks, sheltered by great hanging branches. In the hollow of a big fleshy plant he discovered some dew to drink and he ate some berries which he just hoped weren't poisonous; then he put his head down on a pile of leaves and fell asleep. He was so tired he wanted to sleep for ever.

He'd hoped, of course, that when he woke up in the morning he'd find that it had all been a terrible dream and that he'd be in his nice warm bed with Darren in the sleeping bag on the floor next to him.

But next morning he woke in the jungle, extremely stiff and miserable; horrible little ants were crawling up the inside of his pyjama trousers – and what was that matted stuff in his hair? Was it dried bird's poo? Ugh! He wished he'd brought a comb. Where on earth was he? He felt hungry and frightened.

Above him was a dense canopy of leaves and branches and, around him, tree trunks, trailing vines and brambles barred his way on all sides. Then a single narrow shaft of sunlight pierced through the trees and, looking up, he saw hundreds of birds perched

above him, all staring down. When they saw him they started to chatter – and the noise was deafening. The twittering and tweeting continued for about five minutes before all the birds took off from their branches and, in a great whirring cloud, flew away.

It was only when they'd gone that Paul remembered the third peanut. If he could understand what those birds were saying then maybe he could find out where he was! And maybe he could find out what had happened to Darren and his family.

But the birds had vanished and he had no idea if he'd see them again. Aimlessly Paul wandered round the clearing, looking for more berries and nuts. Normally round this time he'd be at school having his dinner. He'd be rushing out to the playground afterwards and looking forward to going home for tea. But now he wondered if he'd ever see his friends again. Or his mum. Or his dad. He tried to hold back the tears as he sat keeping watch for the birds' return. And then, at midday, they came back.

Excitedly Paul put his hand in his pocket and seized the third and last peanut. He popped it into his mouth and listened. It worked.

"Oh, look, that poor boy's here again," one bird was saying.

"What's he doing?" said another. "He must be lost. If we leave him here he'll die."

"It's such a shame, he'd make a lovely pet," said another. "Maybe we ought to fly to that new place, you know, the Human Zoo, and let them know he's here? Then they could look after him properly."

The Human Zoo! The words gave Paul a terrible shock. Had he heard right? He shouted up, "Did you say the Human Zoo?"

The fact that he could speak their language caused a great deal of surprised chattering in the branches.

"I've never heard a human who can speak in bird language!"

"Isn't that amazing!"

"Did you hear that!"

Above him they all looked most astonished and flapped their wings nervously and hopped uncomfortably about on the branches.

Paul explained. "I was given some magic peanuts by a monkey in the zoo in the town where I live," he called. "I'm here because some animals kidnapped my family and friend in the middle of last night and I managed to escape. I must find them. Can you help me?"

"If he was given magic peanuts, he must be OK," said one bird, flying down and perching on Paul's head.

"Yes, animals only give magic peanuts to humans who love animals," said another, fluttering down. And soon the whole flock was all around Paul, sitting on his arms, his legs, his shoulders, his hair – everywhere. Those that didn't have any room on Paul's body crowded along nearby branches and on the grass.

"What's your name?", "Where do you come from?", "What's the zoo you talked about in your town?", "Are the animals happy there?", "How did you escape being caught?"

The questions came thick and fast as Paul explained the whole story. But when he got to the bit about his family and Darren being driven off in the wagon he burst into tears. "And I don't know where they've gone and I may never see them again," he sobbed.

"The Human Zoo," said the one on his head who seemed to be the leader. "Definitely. It's a whole new thing. We've never had one before. They're advertising the opening today with a family on view. That'll be yours."

It all sounded too horrible and Paul, who'd tried hard to stop crying, felt the tears coming back again.

"But what am I going to do?" he wailed. "I don't even know where it is and even if I did know, how could I get to see them? The animals there would only take me prisoner and put me into a cage as well!"

The birds all started gossiping to each other. Paul had to put his hands over his ears because the noise was so loud, but he could still make out a few words and phrases like, "feathers", "disguise", "show him the way", "but at a price", "conditions".

"How many more peanuts have you got?" asked the one on his head, eventually.

"None," said Paul, looking up. But, as he tilted his head upwards, the bird disappeared from sight. He felt a scrabbling of little claws as the bird tried to regain its balance. Then they all started chattering again. Finally the one on his head hopped down and confronted him. It was a small bird with a bright glossy brown coat with tinges of green in its wing feathers. Its beak was sharp and yellow but its eyes were black, sparkling – and friendly.

"We've got an idea," it said. "But it's dangerous. And we'll only help you if you promise one thing."

"Anything!" said Paul, leaning forward eagerly.

"You've got to promise to show us where the zoo is in your town so we can rescue the animals there."

"But of *course* I will," said Paul. "I'd give anything to help those poor animals!"

"Good lad," said the bird. "Right, here's our plan."

It wasn't very comfortable, Paul decided after a couple of hours, being a bird. That was how long it took for the birds to find enough feathers between them to cover Paul completely. They made a beak for him out of a piece of old bark, and stuck leaves on to his legs to look like scaly skin. They got him to bend his arms like wings and showed him how to flap them to look as if he could fly if he wanted to.

"You do look a bit odd," said the Chief Bird eventually, cocking its head as it stared at him. "But you look more like a bird than a human, that's for sure."

"Of course, you can't fly," said another helpfully. "Your body's too heavy. If any animal asks why you're not flying, you'd better say you've broken a wing."

Paul nodded miserably. The feathers were itchy and there were all kinds of little ticks and fleas from them that crawled uncomfortably about his body. The leaves on his legs tickled and it was hard walking with his feet covered by the moss and twigs that had been designed to look like claws.

"Now, follow us and we'll take you to the Human Zoo," said the Chief Bird. "We bought a ticket for you." It looked just like a leaf to Paul but he took it in his beak with difficulty and walked ahead. As he moved, the birds roared with laughter. "Not like that!" they said. "You look ridiculous! Can't you hop?"

Weighed down with feathers and bark, Paul felt really stupid, but he had a go and with the help of the Chief Bird, practised hopping along a track until finally he came to the edge of the jungle.

"The zoo's that way," said the bird, pointing with its wing. "Once you've got everyone free, bring them back here. Then we'll rescue the animals in your zoo. And then we'll help you back home. Good luck!"

They were going to leave him here all on

his own! But he didn't know where he was or what he was supposed to do. Paul looked helplessly at the Chief Bird but it had its beak under its wing, chasing some horrible creepy-crawly, no doubt, Paul thought bitterly. He'd just have to hope for the best and keep his fingers crossed – not that he seemed to have any fingers any more; they were all glued up with feathers. "I just hope it works out," he added nervously.

"Take care! See you later – I hope!" said the Chief Bird – and flew off.

"But how will I free them? And how will I find my way back?" called Paul, desperately. But now the Chief Bird was just a dot in the sky. Paul was on his own.

With rather lumbering jumps, Paul hopped in the direction of the zoo. When he reached the entrance he found an old elephant standing at the gate. Awkwardly, Paul held out the ticket.

"Thank you, sir," said the elephant, taking the ticket with his trunk. "Come to see the

humans have you? A fascinating experience.
Enjoy your day."

Ahead was a path down which were
wandering families of giraffes, antelope, seals,

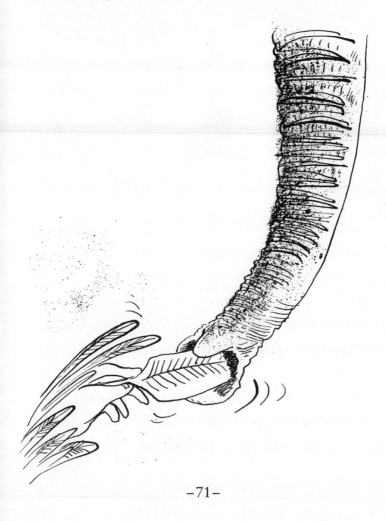

cockroaches, polar bears, crocodiles, bats and
sea-lions – every animal you could think of.
The young animals were skipping and
gambolling about, eating berries and sweet
shoots that were on sale at little kiosks made
of palm leaves. With nervous hops, Paul
followed a series of arrows until he found the
one he wanted. But as he read it, his heart
sank and he gave a rather un-bird-like groan.
For there, written in animal language, were

the words: TO THE GIRL AND BOY. He
looked around nervously. But none of the
other animals seemed to have noticed his
reaction – nor, indeed, did they notice that he
was a rather odd sort of animal. True, one
small ant-eater had pointed to him, and said
in a loud voice, "Look at that funny bird!"
but his mother had given him a hasty slap
and whispered, "Sssh! It's rude to point! Poor
bird, he was probably born like that!"

Screwing up his courage, Paul hopped in the direction of the arrows – and eventually found himself in front of a cage. And inside the cage were Darren and Tricia.

Darren was in one corner, shivering in his pyjamas. After he'd got over the initial shock and relief at seeing them there, Paul couldn't understand why Darren was shivering, as it was so hot. But then it was probably fear rather than cold that made him tremble. In another corner, Tricia was quivering in her nightdress. Between them was a huge pile of very cold chips and, leaning against the wall, was an old bicycle with no tyres on it. It

made Paul's heart ache to see his sister like this. If only he could shout out and tell her he was there! But that would have given the game away. He could only stare dumbly at her through the bars.

Beside him stood a family of kangaroos, the smallest of which clutched a bag of boiled sweets. Every thirty seconds he threw one into the cage.

"Go on," said the father kangaroo. "Throw another one. They say they like boiled sweets." The floor of the cage was littered with unopened boiled sweets.

"They've got some food already," complained the small kangaroo, staring at the chips. "Ugh, I wouldn't like to eat those!"

"Yes, that's their dinner. Chips. Humans like chips. They have them for breakfast, lunch and tea."

"What's that?" asked the small kangaroo, pointing to the bicycle.

"That's for them to get exercise," said the mother kangaroo. "If we're lucky we'll see them riding it. They're meant to be riding at five o'clock."

At this very moment an enormous bear pushed open the door of the cage. He was wielding a big stick and he growled loudly at Darren and Tricia who rushed together and clung to each other.

"Oh, look, isn't that sweet! They're hugging each other!" said a tiger.

With his stick, the bear pushed at Darren, nudging him towards the bike. Darren refused to leave Tricia until the bear grunted, "Get on the bike, you stupid human! Get a move on!" and jabbed at him again. Paul was horrified. He knew Darren couldn't understand what the bear was saying. Eventually, with more poking and pushing, the bear forced Darren on to the bike – and he made a sorry

sight, riding round and round the cage on this broken old machine in his pyjamas.

Meanwhile Tricia was poking around among the sweets and finally picked one, undid the paper and put the sweet into her mouth.

"Look at that! That was your sweet!" said the father kangaroo pointing it out to his son. "And did you see how he peeled it!"

He? The kangaroos were talking about his sister! Paul suddenly heard himself saying, "But that one's a girl!"

"Oh, is it?" said the father kangaroo, turning round and eyeing Paul suspiciously up and down. "And how do you know? Are you an expert?"

"I – er – I just think it is," said Paul, wishing he'd never spoken. "Maybe I'm wrong."

"No, she's right," said a monkey. She! But Paul was a he! Those wretched birds had obviously disguised him as a female! But he kept quiet. The monkey continued. "The males have those long things covering each of their legs and the females have one long piece over them both. Or is it the other way round?"

"Maybe we'll see them mating," said a giraffe behind Paul. "That would be interesting."

Mating! Darren and Tricia! In front of all these animals! Paul felt like turning round and punching the giraffe on the nose, but the giraffe's nose was too high up and anyway it wouldn't be a good idea.

Darren finally got off the bike, hobbled up to the bars and looked around. Tricia came up behind him and stared out.

"Where are Mum and Dad?" whispered Tricia, unhappily. "How long will we have to stay in here?"

"For ever I shouldn't wonder," said Darren. "I can't see how we could escape." A small parrot threw a boiled sweet at Darren which hit him on the nose. All the animals roared with laughter and one reached over and rattled at the bars. Darren put his hands over his ears to block out the noise of animals laughing.

"Oh, look, isn't he sweet, he's washing his ears!" squeaked a penguin.

Tricia wandered wearily back to her seat and sighed. "We can't stay here for ever. We'll die of boredom. And we can't live on chips and boiled sweets. They seem to think that's all we eat."

"What happened to Paul?" asked Darren, in a low voice.

"I don't know," said Tricia, starting to cry and putting her hands to her eyes. "Oh, I hope he's OK. I hope they haven't eaten him! Oh, to think I might never see him again! My little brother!"

Was that really his sister speaking? Paul couldn't believe his ears. He'd never heard Tricia talk like that about him before. At home she was always complaining about him – but here she was actually missing him! A lump came to his throat.

"Now *she*'s washing her *face*!" said a seal.

"Yes," said the seal's father. "You see, humans have special water in their eyes and when they want to wash their faces they let it out and they rub their faces with it to clean themselves."

Paul shook his head. The animals had absolutely no idea about how humans lived or felt – no more idea, he felt guiltily, than the keepers at the zoo back home had about how the animals really lived.

Still, he couldn't waste time thinking. How to rescue them – that was the big question.

The only exit was the cage door which was
tied with a big piece of knotted grass – a knot
that looked too difficult for a human to undo.
Maybe when the bear next came to feed them
Paul could slip in and let them out. But how
would he deal with the bear? His mind
boggled. Maybe his dad would have an idea.

Despite feeling awful about leaving Tricia
and Darren without somehow letting them
know that help was at hand, Paul pulled
himself together and hopped down a path to
find his parents. He passed several stalls
selling mangoes and shoots of leaves before

he found a sign saying: HUMAN – MALE.

How could they describe his dad like that? His dad was someone who took him to football matches, who used to lift him up on to his shoulders so he could see; his dad was the one who always winked at him behind Mum's back when she complained about his untidy room; his dad was always planning outings and surprises and he was always cracking jokes. No way could his dad be summed up as simply: HUMAN – MALE.

Paul followed the signs until he came to a dark passage. Stumbling down it, he found another cage, lit by a small hole in the roof that let in a faint glow of daylight. It was only when his eyes became accustomed to the darkness that he could make out someone inside. His father was sitting on the floor in his pyjamas. Opposite him was a weird box made of wood. It was shaped, very crudely, like a television.

"What's that, Dad?" asked a frog in the audience, peering in.

"That, son, is something that these humans like watching in the dark. We don't quite understand why, but they seem to enjoy it." His froggy father clearly enjoyed giving his son the benefit of his knowledge. He gave a satisfied croak at the end of his little speech.

"Can I throw him a cigarette?" asked the frog who was holding a packet.

"Yes, of course," said the father frog. "Most human men need cigarettes to keep them alive. No one knows why." Paul felt like screaming. His dad had just given up, with the utmost difficulty! And what was his father feeling, watching that empty box when there weren't even any programmes on it? Sitting there, he was clearly in a state of complete shock. But when the cigarette came flying in, he leapt up in a mad rage and seized the bars, rattling them furiously. "Let me out! Let me out!" he yelled. "And where's my wife and family? You can't do this to me!"

"Oh, isn't he having fun!" said an elephant. It trumpeted back at him.

Paul's father became more and more enraged. "Let me out! Help! Help!"

Then the elephant did something awful. It put its trunk into a small pool and sprayed Paul's dad all over. Paul's dad fell backwards with the blast of water and got up, staggering and moaning.

"He's having a game with us!" shouted a camel. "Oh, he liked that! Do it again!"

Unable to bear a moment longer, Paul hopped quickly back down the dark passage, determined to find his mum. The next signpost read: HUMAN – FEMALE and he

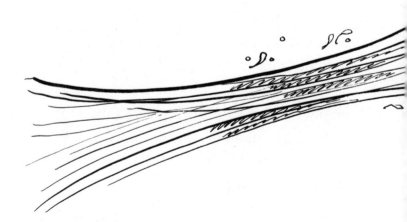

rushed along the path as fast as he could. He had almost forgotten to hop now, in his haste. There was no time to be wasted. Luckily, the animals were so interested in enjoying their day out and looking at the humans that they didn't take much notice of him.

Finding his mum was almost the worst experience of all. Like his father, she was alone in a cage – but she was just sitting on the earth floor crying quietly. Paul had only once seen his mum crying – when he'd got lost in a big shop and had finally been returned to her after half an hour in the manager's office – and he was shocked. Her nightdress was torn and her bun had come adrift.

"She's singing!" said a rabbit. "Listen! She must be happy!"

"Let's throw her some of these!" said a tortoise, producing a lipstick from under his shell. "She'll like that. Human females like putting these on their mouths and then licking the stuff off. It's very odd."

He threw the lipstick into the cage but Paul's mother just looked at it in despair. "Oh, where am I? And where's my family? Oh, Tricia, Paul ... where are you?"

The animals round his mother's cage had got bored and started drifting away. At last Paul was on his own! Now he could let his mum know he was there. Leaning forward, he pushed his beak through the bars.

"Go away!" screamed his mother. "Stop it! Don't come any further!"

"Mum!" whispered Paul through his bark beak. "Calm down! It's me, Paul!"

His mother stared at him. "Paul! Surely not!" Her eyes were practically popping out of her head with astonishment.

"Yes, it *is* me, Mum," said Paul. "I've been helped by some friends!"

"What friends? And what have they done to you! You're covered with feathers! They've changed you into a bird! Oh, darling, what's going on! Where are we?"

"No, it's just a disguise," whispered Paul impatiently. "I'm me underneath! I'll explain later. There's no time to lose."

His mother clung on to the bars pathetically, reaching out to stroke his feathers and his beak. "But are these friends of yours to be trusted?" she whispered. "You can't risk getting caught yourself. You should go back home now – then at least one of us will be safe. Take Tricia and Darren with you if you can, but leave Dad and me. Don't risk it. We've had a life but you're young and have got your future before you!" And with that a tear trickled down her cheek.

"Shut up!" said Paul to his mother, sharply – and for once she didn't tick him off. "You're talking rubbish! I couldn't go away leaving you here! Don't be so stupid! Now," he said, trying to sound efficient, "I'll hide here for a while until the zoo closes, and then I'll come back and we'll try to find a way of getting you all out of here and back to the jungle."

And at that very moment an animal announced over a loudspeaker, "The Human Zoo is closing in five minutes. Please make your way to the exit. The Human Zoo is closing in five minutes. We hope you enjoyed your day. Please return tomorrow – and bring your friends!"

Trying to blow his mother a rather crisp kiss through his barky beak, Paul hurried

away, hopping down a path until he found a
cave full of sacks of boiled sweets, cigarettes
and lipsticks – stores of stuff for the animals
to throw at the humans. Crouching down, he
hid as best he could and waited till it got dark.

So far, so good. But if only he had a plan!

He heard the sounds of the kiosk owners
packing up for the night, and the shouts of

"Goodbye" from the various zoo-keepers and staff as they left for their homes. Through the entrance of the cave, Paul could see the stars slowly coming out one by one; then the whole place was filled with an eerie silence broken only by the sounds of Tricia calling out, "Mum! Mum!" But through the darkness Paul could also hear the padding footsteps of the one keeper on duty, the big bear who patrolled the cages regularly, puffing and grunting.

Now was the time, Paul knew, to set his family free. But how was he going to do it?

Chapter Five

Paul's feathered suit was getting terribly hot.
It would have been nice to take it off –
because after all, if he were caught helping
his family escape, it wouldn't make much
difference whether he were a bird or a
human. But then he decided not to risk it. He
could stop hopping now, because that would
delay him, but he'd keep his feathers on.

When he thought it was safe, he crept out
of the cave and tiptoed slowly down the path.
There was no sound except the odd shrieking
of some strange night-time warbler and the
occasional screaming of a hyena in the
distance. The air was dank and humid,

pressing in on Paul and making him feel even more uncomfortable. Some religions said that when you died, you returned to earth again – perhaps as a fish or an insect. Paul made a mental note to insist that he would *not* return as a bird. It just wasn't his thing.

It would probably be best, he thought to himself, to get Mum first. She was nearest – and it was, anyway, unbearable to think of her so unhappy. When he arrived at her cage, she was sitting on top of a pile of leaves waiting for him. The moment she spotted him, she jumped up and came rushing over to the bars. "Oh, darling!" she whispered. "You're safe! But how can we get me out? I've been checking the knot on the door and I don't think either of us has the strength to undo it."

Paul wriggled his arms free of his feathery wings and examined the grassy rope in the darkness, tugging at it and wiggling it – but to no avail. "If only I had a knife I could cut it at once." He pulled at it in frustration.

"But of course they don't have knives here," whispered his mum. "Isn't there anything else we could use?"

They looked around – but there was nothing. His mum's plate of old chips wouldn't help as the plate was just a big palm leaf. The only other things were the lipsticks on the floor of her cage.

"That's metal," Paul said, getting an idea. He pointed to the casing of the lipsticks. "Look, if you jumped on one of those and squeezed it flat, wouldn't the cover break and make a kind of rough edge for us to saw with?"

It was difficult for his mother to squash down the lipstick with her bare feet but, after a great deal of jumping, one of the lipstick casings flattened. Then it was a matter of simply wrestling with it to weaken the metal until it finally broke in two.

Between them, each using one half, they managed to saw through the grassy rope until it broke, the two ragged edges falling away to enable Paul's mum to push open the door and step into her son's arms. Until they hugged each other, Paul hadn't quite realized how much he'd missed his mum. All of a sudden, as he felt her arms round his feathery suit, he seemed to become about three years old. It felt so marvellous to be with each other, it was an effort to remember that the task was far from over.

"I just can't believe it," his mum kept saying. "To think you're so clever! But who are these friends of yours who helped you? And how did you escape?"

"No time to explain," whispered Paul. "I'll tell you later. Now we've got to free Dad and Tricia and Darren."

Mum lifted her nightie as she stepped along the path. Then, fed up, she leaned down, ripped a strip off the bottom and tied it round her waist to make it shorter.

If only he could remember the way to his father's cage, thought Paul as he led her along. It was so dark – and he was so frightened they might meet the bear – that his

memory played tricks on him and he took constant wrong turnings.

But at last the sign saying HUMAN – MALE appeared, and Paul guided his mother down the dark passage to where his father was kept prisoner.

"Dad!" he whispered. But his father, just a dark shape in the middle of the cage, was fast asleep, exhausted by the horror of the day. "Dad!"

"Wake up, love!" whispered Mum through the bars. "It's us!" But still he wouldn't wake up. Paul's mum found a long grass and stuck it through the bars, tickling him.

"Go away!" grunted Dad, rolling over grumpily. "Go away and leave me! I can't stand any more!"

"Dad!" whispered Paul. "It's me!"

Suddenly there was a rustling sound as Dad jerked up his head and stared into the darkness. "Who's that?" he whispered suspiciously.

"It's me, Paul!" said Paul.

"PAUL?" said his dad, jumping up in amazement. "But – but – it can't be!" As he came towards the bars he rubbed his eyes and peered out. When he saw Paul in his bird suit he shrank back.

Then Mum spoke. "It's Paul, love!" she whispered. "He's disguised. We've come to set you free!"

His dad's look changed to one of smiling astonishment as he heard Mum's voice. "Darling!" he said. Paul had never heard him call Mum "darling" before. "My love!"

"Come on," said Paul, getting impatient and handing his dad half the broken lipstick casing. "Here's a kind of knife we made out of lipsticks – can you saw the knot on your side of the cage door? It'll be quicker."

Within minutes his father was free. He leapt out of the cage and put his arms round both of them, giving them the biggest squeeze in the world.

"Paul, you are amazing!" Dad's voice shook in the darkness. "How on earth did you do it? How did you escape? I never in a million years imagined…" Now his dad was free at last. He'd know what to do. Paul was exhausted, as if he could quite easily just lie down right on the spot and go to sleep, letting Dad take over.

Dad hugged Paul even tighter. "You feel so odd," he added. "All feathery! I just can't get over this! You escaped and came to rescue us! Paul, you're the best and most brilliant son in the world!"

"Come on," said Mum. "There's no time to lose! We've still got to get Darren and Tricia."

Paul's dad gave Mum a great big kiss. "I can't believe you're safe! I've been imagining..."

But as he spoke, a crunch of footsteps down the passageway made their hearts stop beating. The bear! With a great bellowing and growling, the furious animal came crashing down the passageway, his white teeth flashing and his black beady eyes sparkling with rage.

"What's going on here!" he roared. His eyes were unaccustomed to the dark and he couldn't see properly.

Realizing he was the only one the bear could understand, Paul took instinctive action. He hopped into his father's cage. "Can't catch me!" he shouted to the bear. "Come and get me!"

The bear lumbered into the cage, his claws out, whereupon Paul nipped through the door and slammed it behind him. "Quick, the grasses!" he said.

"But that's no good, Paul – he can undo them," said Dad. "He'll be able to get out! We'll have to run for it!"

The three of them sped down the passageway and out into the open. The bear's thundering footsteps behind them made Paul quake with fear. Even worse, he was roaring, "I'll get you! I'll eat you for breakfast! You can't escape!"

"Up that tree!" whispered Paul's dad, pointing. "He'd never think of looking for a human up a tree!"

"But Dad, bears are always climbing trees!" protested Paul. "Let's jump into that pond! He won't go in there!" The family struggled through giant bullrushes and managed to conceal themselves in the swampy depths of a particularly smelly pool. Paul closed his eyes and held on to Dad's hand tightly; he just

hoped there weren't any crocodiles awake at that time of night. Meanwhile the bear had emerged furiously from the passage. Sure enough, although he looked everywhere – even up the tree – he didn't look into the pool, and eventually he charged off down the path that led to Paul's mother's cage.

When they got to Tricia and Darren, Dad set to work at once with the lipstick casing. The atmosphere of fear and haste was nerve-racking. Paul kept thinking his heart would jump out of his mouth he felt so terrified. What if they failed? Would the bear eat them? Or would he be captured along with his family to live in the zoo for ever? And if so, who'd help them then?

Luckily there was no time to think, and as Darren and Tricia woke up at the sound of their door being shaken, Dad silenced their questions with, "We'll explain later!"

"But who's that horrible bird thing with you?" asked Tricia, pointing to Paul. "And where's Paul?"

"Where's your lipstick bit?" Dad suddenly asked Paul. "Mine's gone blunt."

Paul felt all over his feathers. Nothing! He'd left it behind in Dad's cage!

"Is there anything in there you could cut with?" asked Paul's dad, staring into his daughter's cage.

"The bicycle!" said Darren. "If I can rip the chain off, or one of the mudguards…"

Between them he and Tricia managed to pull the bicycle apart and with the chain Paul's dad tore the fastening grasses to shreds.

There was no time for hugs and kisses; they could hear the bear behind them, growling and muttering to himself.

Stooping low and creeping along as fast as possible, the family followed Paul as he led them to the exit, climbed over the fence and escaped into a field. Tricia's nightdress was torn, and Paul, Mum and Dad were soaked from hiding in the pond. Paul's feathers were dripping and he looked a very sorry, mad bird indeed. As they ran, the sounds of the bear, still padding round the zoo looking for his captives, grew fainter and fainter.

"This way!" said Paul and together they ran down a path towards the jungle. But they were running so fast and it was so dark that they didn't notice a group of animals talking to each other in a clearing.

A huge vulture, one of the group, put out a wing to halt their escape. "Not so fast!" it cawed. "Stop!"

This was the last thing they needed. Paul's mother screamed and his father clenched his

fists as if preparing to fight. Tricia burst into tears and Darren stood absolutely still, frozen with fear.

"Yes?" said Paul. The only way out of this was to stay as cool as possible. To his family he hissed, "Shut up!"

"What are you doing out in the middle of the night?" the vulture asked Paul. "And who

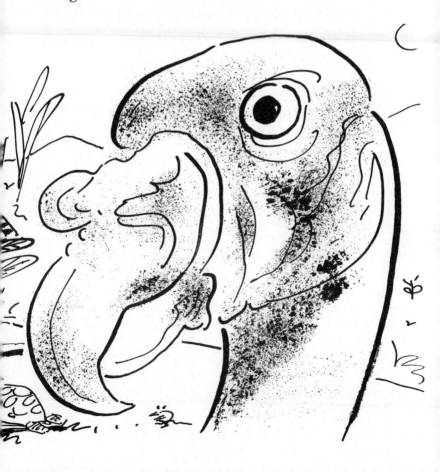

are you, and who are these humans you've got with you?"

"Humans? Humans?" Paul's mind raced. "Oh, so you were fooled by my friends' costumes! Great! We've just come from a fancy dress party and I'm – er – disguised as a kind of mythical bird and my friends here decided to dress up as humans."

"Dress up!" A kangaroo emerged from a bush and examined Tricia's skin very closely. "It's a very good costume, if I may say so. Looks real to me."

"Yes, yes…" Paul chattered on. "But they're not real humans, you know. This one here is an – an – ostrich." He pointed to his mother.

"How did it manage to get its feet like that, then?" asked a turtle suspiciously.

"Amazing, just – er – folded over. Very uncomfortable. Got to get back quickly to change."

"And this?" The vulture pointed to Darren.

"A sparrow," burbled Paul. "An extremely

big and extremely strong sparrow. Inside the human suit. Amazing isn't it? Um, ah, this is an elephant," he said, pointing to Tricia. "A very, very tiny elephant. Must get it back to bed soon."

"Where's its trunk?"

"Oh, ah, kind of folded away in its face. Very small trunk of course."

"And this, this human male?" asked an ant-eater staring at Paul's dad and looking carefully at his hands.

"It's a horse. Or rather, it's a pony. A Shetland pony. A miniature Shetland pony. Hooves all tucked up inside, you see."

"Amazing," said the vulture, shaking its head as it goggled at them all. "Good party, was it? Wish I'd been there."

"Yes, yes, very good." Paul prattled on as fast as he could. "To celebrate the opening of the Human Zoo, you know. Brilliant. You've seen it?"

"No, but I've heard of it," said a mouse. "I'm going tomorrow."

"Allow me to present you with some free tickets," said Paul in a fit of inspiration. He pulled out ten bedraggled feathers from his chest and handed them round. "Tell them the bear sent you."

"You're a bear under that bird suit?" exclaimed a pigeon. "I've never seen anything like it."

"Amazing what a good fancy dress can do," said Paul, attempting a growl. "Still, must be going. Lovely to meet you. Have a good day tomorrow." And off he hopped followed by his mum, dad, Tricia and Darren, leaving the astonished group of animals behind them.

They didn't stop till they got way, way into the jungle. Through bushes, past streams and waterfalls, past brambles and trailing vines they clambered, until at last they reached Paul's clearing. The birds had stayed up and had prepared a meal of berries and flowers – and they were so hungry it all tasted delicious.

"So what's the plan?" asked Paul's dad at the end of the meal when Paul had told

everyone the whole story. "The birds are going to help the animals back home escape, right?"

"I must say," said Mum, "I had no idea how awful it was being kept in a zoo."

"It's *terrible*!" said Darren. And Dad agreed. "I just don't know what I was talking about when I said I wouldn't mind living in a zoo," he said. "It's so easy to say it but you never think about what it's really like."

"No," said Tricia. "And thanks to Paul we're free at last. You really are clever, Paul."

At this point the Chief Bird came hopping up and spoke to Paul. "Right," it said. "Tomorrow you can show us the way to the zoo, and then we'll plan how to help our friends. And I think you'll need an extra peanut for tomorrow because if I'm not mistaken, the effects of that last one will be wearing off pretty soon." And the bird was right, because as it produced a final peanut from under its wing, Paul found that he couldn't make any more sense of what it was saying. All he could hear was a chorus of comforting tweets and chatters and chirrups as they all settled down for the night.

The next morning the sun was pouring through the leaves of the jungle and the birds were gossiping noisily above. Dad, still in his pyjamas and unshaven, looked much more cheerful. Mum had re-assembled her bun with twigs. Darren and Tricia were joking with each other, and Paul, who'd managed to unglue the last feather from himself, felt a lot more comfortable. As the Chief Bird hopped down and spoke, Paul popped the peanut into his mouth.

"I hope you're all feeling better after yesterday," it said to Paul. "Your family certainly *looks* a lot happier. Though I think they should have a good day's rest here before setting off for home. They'll be suffering from shock."

"Oh, thanks," said Paul. "But I'm fine. Can we set off for the zoo?"

"Straight away," said the Chief Bird. "A few of the birds will stay here to look after your family, but the rest are coming with us. You'll be riding on our backs so I hope you're not frightened of heights."

"Won't I fall off?" asked Paul, worriedly.

"Not if you hold on tightly," said the Chief Bird, signalling for some of the others to fly down.

Eventually about a dozen of the strongest birds lined themselves up on the ground and Paul sat gingerly down on their backs. There was a great whirring of wings and slowly he felt himself being lifted off the ground and up above the trees. "See you soon!" he called to his family.

"Take care, Paul!" called his mum.

"Good luck!" called his dad.

"Fasten your seatbelt!" yelled Darren.

And Tricia just waved and waved and blew kisses until soon the whole family became tiny dots and eventually disappeared as Paul felt himself being lifted high, high up into the

air surrounded by a veritable army of birds.

After about half an hour the lush scenery beneath him disappeared and was replaced by more magnificent views – mountain ranges, rivers, seas, hills, rocky passes and low flat plains. Because they were so high up, the wind was cold, but the sun beat on his face, warming him, as they passed through clouds and mists and rainstorms and sunbursts until suddenly he could see familiar buildings and roads below.

"There it is!" he shouted, pointing excitedly. And the birds, following his directions, slowly flew lower and lower until they landed with a big bump on a patch of green grass in the middle of the zoo.

It was too early for any of the keepers to be up and about but all the animals seemed curiously expectant. When the birds started to discuss their next move, Paul took the opportunity to walk around and speak to his friends.

"You'll soon all be free," he whispered to the monkey who'd given him the magic peanuts in the first place. "The birds are going to take you back to … to the jungle." He didn't really know where they'd been over the last couple of days; it certainly didn't seem like a country with a name. After all there had been penguins and polar bears there alongside kangaroos and lions, and he distinctly remembered seeing an Indian elephant and an African elephant sitting side by side on a bench at the Human Zoo.

Perhaps it was a country as magical as the peanuts he'd been given – and yet it had all been real enough. Horribly real. But his attention was distracted by the monkey dancing up and down in its cage with delight; it even tried to give him a rubbery kiss through the bars.

"I'll be swinging from the trees in the jungle with all my friends and gathering fruit – yippee!" it yelled. "Paul, you're a genius! The moment I set eyes on you, I knew that you were a true friend of the animals!" Then it rushed back to spread the good news.

"You'll soon be free," Paul told the giraffe when he'd explained the birds' plan.

The giraffe looked up to the sky with a look of rapture. "I'll gallop along the plains with a great herd of other giraffes, tasting the sweet shoots on the trees! Bliss!"

"You'll soon be soaring the skies," Paul told the eagle, who clapped its wings together and squawked in reply, "You mean I'll really be feeling the wind through my feathers at last? Wonderful!"

And the dolphins leapt and splashed with delight when they found out that it would only be a matter of hours before they'd be back in the great blue ocean, swimming free on the crests of the waves as the seagulls cawed above them.

"You'll see your family again," Paul told the elephant – and the polar bear was so thrilled when it heard the news that it skidded down its concrete rock into the muddy pool.

Only the lion was disbelieving. "It's impossible," he said, mournfully. "I'll never see my homeland again. I'm resigned to it."

Then suddenly everything became dark. Looking up, Paul saw that the whole flock of birds had gathered above the zoo. The sky just got darker and darker as the birds, thousands and thousands of them, descended. They flew in and out of the cages, until everything went black.

Then, when it grew lighter, he saw that all the animals were being carried into the sky by the birds. As Paul was lifted along with them he noticed that they even managed to get the elephant up, though for the whole journey back to the jungle Paul could see that the birds carrying the huge beast were puffing and panting and flew much lower than everyone else.

As all the animals in the zoo were carried
along through the clouds they started singing.

"Hurrah, hurrah, hurrah for Paul,
He's the best human of them all,
We're going home to have a ball,
Hurrah, hurrah, hurrah for Paul!"

The old monkey couldn't sing in tune but it
clapped its furry hands, slapping its palms
together in time. Occasionally, when its
feelings overwhelmed it, it leapt over the raft
of birds to slap Paul on the back and plant a

big monkey kiss on his cheek. As a gesture of supreme friendship it started picking at Paul's hair, examining it for ticks and lice. And even though it tickled, Paul felt it would be too rude to ask it to stop.

Eventually they arrived at the jungle clearing and slowly descended to the ground as Paul's mum and dad, Tricia and Darren all clapped and cheered.

The moment it landed on the ground, the giraffe immediately reached up to nibble the sweet shoots at the top of the trees; the polar bear raced off to slide down an iceberg; the elephant trumpeted for joy as a whole group of elephant friends came stampeding into the jungle to welcome it home. The eagle took off with a great flapping of wings and surveyed the scene from the sky, while the dolphins splashed in the water of a nearby lake. The lion gave a triumphant roar and bounded off into the undergrowth, to emerge a little later to sit on a rock above them, in the sun, roaring with ecstasy as he overlooked the happy scene.

The big old monkey stayed with Paul and, in front of all the animals, shook his hand in its monkey hand. "If it hadn't been for you, we'd never have escaped," said the monkey, tears coming into its beady old eyes. "We just can't thank you enough."

At this point a rabbit popped up from a hole in the ground and squeaked, "Yes, Paul! I haven't burrowed into the soft earth for two years, and it's absolutely brilliant! Thanks!"

"And on behalf of all the animals," continued the monkey, "I'd like to present you with the order of the Freedom of the Jungle."

"Thanks ever so much," said Paul, feeling a little bit shy. "But honestly, it was nothing. The birds did all the work."

"I know they did, but without your help, help from a human, they'd never have found the zoo. It just goes to show that we all need each other, animals and humans. So now I'm going to give you this – " and the monkey tugged a little bit of loose brown fur from its coat and handed it to Paul – "and whenever you want to come back and see us, all you have to do is to rub it against your cheek and you'll be back here in a jiffy, speaking our language and always certain of a friendly welcome."

"Well that's better than being a zoo-keeper!" said Paul, taking the precious tuft of fur and putting it carefully into his pyjama pocket. "Thanks ever so much, monkey. That's the nicest birthday present of all!"

The Chief Bird was coughing a kind of tweeting bird-like cough. If it had had a watch to look at it would have consulted it. "I'm sorry to interrupt," it said, "but it's getting late and the birds are very tired and really we'd like to take you and your family home now so we can get back before nightfall. Would you mind?"

"Not at all," said Paul. "You've been so kind to help me and my family. It's all been brilliant."

The Chief Bird's feathers went a little bit red. "OK then? Ready for lift-off?"

Paul, Paul's mum and dad, and Tricia and Darren all clambered on to the birds' backs and slowly rose into the air.

"Goodbye!" called Paul to the monkey.

"Goodbye, Paul!" called the monkey. "Come back and see us soon, won't you?"

"I will!" said Paul. The eagle flew with them a little way, the elephant trumpeted in farewell, the lion roared, the dolphins splashed in the water, the giraffe craned its

head right up to see them leave and the polar bear did a double somersault down its iceberg.

"Oh, it's sad to leave them, isn't it?" said Paul's mum. "They were ever so nice." And she dabbed at her eyes with a corner of her nightdress.

"But it's even nicer to see them so happy rather than in the zoo," said Paul's dad.

They flew and flew and flew over the same extraordinary landscape as before, until finally, Paul's dad pointed. "Look, there's the golf course by my office!" he said.

"And there's my school!" said Darren, staring down. "I can't wait to get back."

"And look at the supermarket where I do my shopping!" cried Mum. "I'll make you all a great big supper tonight!"

Paul looked down and waited till he could see their house. After all his adventures, the only place he really wanted to be was home.

They landed on the outskirts of the town and, saying an emotional goodbye to the

Chief Bird and their other bird friends, they slowly walked back home – keeping to the back streets because they were still in their pyjamas and nightdresses.

Suddenly Darren put a finger to his lips. "Listen!" he said.

From an open window they could hear the sound of radio news. The newscaster sounded serious. "In a mystery incident today, all the animals escaped from the zoo," he said. "The owners confess it is an inexplicable occurrence. One of them said tonight, 'We are completely ruined. We will never be able to replace all the animals so we have decided to put the whole zoo up for sale as a new housing development.'"

Everyone grinned and gave each other thumbs up signs. When they got home, and Mum had made a lovely big supper and Darren had rung his parents to tell them he was safe and sound and Paul's dad had explained to his office that he'd been ill with flu (they'd never have believed the real story); Paul said, "In the end, and despite everything, that was the nicest birthday treat I've ever had."

And he thought of the polar bear sliding into its arctic pool, the giraffe running swiftly over the grasslands, the rabbits burrowing into the earth, the dolphins leaping and playing in the sea, the eagle soaring in the sky, the lion sitting in the sunshine on a rock overlooking the plains, lord of all he surveyed and, best of all, the monkey swinging from branch to branch, from tree to tree for miles and miles in the jungle. He felt in his pocket for the little tuft of fur and knew that one day he'd certainly go back and pay them a visit.

After all, they were his friends.